Henry Todd

North Country Ballads

Henry Todd

North Country Ballads

ISBN/EAN: 9783744787383

Printed in Europe, USA, Canada, Australia, Japan

Cover: Foto ©Andreas Hilbeck / pixelio.de

More available books at **www.hansebooks.com**

NORTH COUNTRY

BALLADS.

BY

HENRY TODD.

LONDON:

HORACE COX,

WINDSOR HOUSE, BREAM'S BUILDINGS, CHANCERY LANE, E.C.

—

1895.

LONDON :

PRINTED BY HORACE COX, WINDSOR HOUSE, BREAM'S BUILDINGS, E.C.

CONTENTS.

An English Thermopylæ .　　.　　.

Heavenfield .　　.　　.　　.　　.

Young Roland .　　.　　.　　.

Bellister　　.　　.　　.　　.　　.　　.

Neville's Cross .　　.　　.　　.

The Mosstroopers　　.　　.

The Plague Ship　　.　　.

Skollo the Dane .　　.　　.　　.

NORTH COUNTRY BALLADS.

AN ENGLISH THERMOPYLÆ.

Now the summer day is done,
Now sinks the summer sun
To his rest behind Helvellyn's bulwark steep :
Strikes the ruddy glory now
On Placefell's lofty brow,
And across the dale the twilight shadows creep.

Now the scythe is laid aside,
Which the sturdy dalesman plied
In the meadows by the Goldrill's water clear :
Now the haymaking is done,
And the crop is housed and won ;
All is over, save the laughter and the cheer.

B

Now to the Joyful Tree
Comes a goodly company,
Intent to dance a merry night away.
Each one laughs as he perceives
In his perch amid the leaves
The fiddler making music loud and gay.

For a while all prospers well;
Then, as though by sudden spell,
Breaks the music in the middle of the air;
Cease the dancers' merry feet
On the grassy sward to beat,
And the song becomes a wailing of despair:

For with breathless terror pale
Comes a man of Matterdale,
And his tidings turn the festival to fear:
"There are border thieves at hand,
Scottish foes are in the land,
And, ere the night be done, will they be here.

Round by Carrock foot they came,
Left Mungrisedale all aflame,
By Troutbeck side no single soul survives;

All the Dockray folk are fled
To the coves of Deepdale Head :
Fly ye also, and ye yet may save your lives."

Out spake William Mounsey then,
" We be thirty stalwart men ;
Shame upon us, if our homes we thus forsake !
Let the bairns and women fly,
While we thirty win or die
In the narrow path betwixt the crag and lake."

And the men with one accord
Brought the bow and spear and sword,
And the women kissed them and refused to fly ;
" Nay," they murmured, " let us stay :
Do you fight, and we will pray :
God will help us : if you live not, we will die."

So they came unto the place,
Down by Stybarrow's rocky base,
Where fronts the crag the lake's sheer-dipping edge;
On one hand the waters deep,
And on one the rugged steep,
And between them but a yard or two of ledge.

Then the valiant Mounsey spake,
As they waited by the lake,
" Here we meet them; they are many we are few
Yet be ye not afraid ;
God will surely grant us aid ;
They are robbers, we are honest men and true."

And they answered, "Here we stand
For our homes and native land,
And here, if duty bid us, do we die ;
Yet we trow the Scotch shall feel
The full burden of our steel
Right sorely, ere a man of them go by."

Came a rumbling sound and low,
That betrayed the coming foe,
And they braced themselves for battle hand to hand
And along the narrow track,
With two hundred at his back,
At a canter came the leader of the band.

Aye, he came, but swift and true
Sped the shaft that pierced him through ;
Down he fell, and lay there writhing like a snake :

Reared the steed in dire affright,
Reared, and backed into the night,
And thrust the next that followed in the lake.

And a loud and joyful shout
From the Englishmen broke out :
For a moment stayed the foe, as if in fear ;
Then they charged upon the sound,
But the dalesmen held their ground,
And stoutly plied the arrow and the spear.

Then each riever backed his horse,
For the ledge's narrow course
Did space for but a single steed afford ;
Yet many a one fell dead,
For the arrows truly sped,
And truly thrust the spear and smote the sword.

Then on foot along the track
Came they wildly pouring back,
With shock of onset terrible and hard :
But Mounsey in the front
Bore the battle's fiercest brunt,
Nor ever could they drive him back a yard.

Raged the fight with fury mad;
But the dalesmen's hearts grew sad;
" The task is all too heavy : we must die."
" Up ! " they cried, " let every man
Fight on, while yet he can ;
And we all must perish, ere we let them by."

Stole three shepherds from the rear,
Laid aside the sword and spear,
And scaled the crag, as flushed the dawning light ;
And thence they plied the bow
On the terror-stricken foe,
And hurled the rocks upon them from the height.

Down the Scotchmen went like grass
In that fatal narrow pass,
And the remnant turned about, and sought to fly.
Then cried Mounsey, " Up ! they break !
Up ! and drive them in the lake !
For the Lord hath bid us live : we shall not die !"

What a slaughter then befell !
'Twere a ghastly tale to tell
How many did the steel, the water, slay ;

How few they were that fled,
Scarce better they than dead,
For the country side was up, and it was day.

So ceased at length the fight,
So ended that dread night :
The stout arm drooped, and ached the bleeding head;
And with weary limbs sore spent
Slowly home the dalesmen went,
But twenty—for the rest were lying dead.

And with wild and mingled shout
Came their wives and children out,
And at the sight they felt their courage break :
Many sobbed in glad relief,
Many wept with bitter grief
For the ten that lay all silent by the lake.

And while Helvellyn stands
Stretching forth his mighty hands
Down toward the flat green meadows of the vale,
While Stybarrow moveth not,
Be the story ne'er forgot
Of the fight that once was fought for Patterdale.

HEAVENFIELD.

UNTO the town of Hagustald there came a word of
    fear,
  " Cadwallon moveth northward, and his rage is as
    the wind :
Saw we hall and homestead burning on the further
    side of Wear,
  Ere we turned to flight, and hitherward he follows
    fast behind.
He hath slain King Eanfrith basely, though he
    humbly craved for peace ;
  And thegn and churl, and wife and child, he
    thirsteth all to slay.
Who shall guide us in our trouble ?   Shall the House
    of Ida cease,
  Of that great king who bore the flame that drove
    his sires away ? "

And from the little city went there up a bitter cry,
  " Odin heedeth us no longer, to the gods we pray
    in vain.
Who can stand against this wizard ? Gather up your
    goods and fly
  To the northward, to the northward, till he turn
    him back again."
So they rose and fled to northward—O the horror of
    that flight,
  The weariness, the hunger, and the ever-spurring
    fear !—
Till they reached the heights of Heavenfield, and
    rested for the night,
  And took counsel all together, for the foe drew
    yet more near.

And half the night they wrangled, nor could one
    advise aright ;
  " Who shall lead us ? " 'Twas a riddle, and the
    answer none could tell ;
Till from the murky background came beneath the
    torches' light
  A noble youth, and on the throng a sudden silence
    fell.

"Ask ye still what man shall lead you?   Will ye
   still to folly cling?
Shall he find you thus divided?   Well ye know
   what cometh then.
I am Oswald, son of Aethelfrith.   Behold, I am your king!
   Behold, I am your leader!   Rise, and quit your-
   selves like men!"

Then spake one, "Thou art a Christian."   But the
   youth upon him turned :
"Where, then, are Thor and Odin gone in this
   your hour of need?
Are your kinsmen yet unslaughtered?   Are your
   homesteads yet unburned?
Would they have let their temples fall, if they were
   gods indeed?
Ye shall leave these useless idols : ye shall seek the
   only One,
The only God that liveth, and Him only shall ye
   trust :
His breath shall smite Cadwallon's host, and, ere a
   day be done,
We shall drive our foes before us, as the wind
   whirls up the dust.

This night I lay in slumber, and a glorious dream I
 dreamed,
 The holy Saint Columba saw I standing by my side;
And with his flowing mantle to enfold our folk he
 seemed,
 And the glory of his presence lit the darkness far
 and wide.
' God loves,' said he, ' this people, and if they to Him
 will turn,
 Though dark and drear the prospect, they shall
 fight and conquer yet.
Cadwallon's headless body shall the meanest of you
 spurn,
 And his power and pride be humbled, ere another
 sun be set.'

Then hearken and take courage.   Shall the work our
 fathers wrought
 Be shattered by a Welshman?   Be ye English,
 stout and true !
God hath not given this country to the English race
 for nought,
 And by your hands some goodly work He purposeth
 to do.''

He spake, and from the gathered throng arose a
    joyful cry,
    " Lead on, lead on to battle !   See, already dawns
    the light.
Lead on, lead on to battle !   We will conquer or will die,
    Thy God shall be our God, if He will aid us in the
    fight."

Then spake Oswald to his captains, " Raise we here
    upon this mound
    The Cross, in token of the faith that shall be yours
    to-day."
And soon a lofty cross of wood was planted in the
    ground,
    And at its foot the monarch knelt, and bowed his
    head to pray.
He knelt and prayed in silence, and at once with one
    accord
    The stern rough heathen warriors knelt humbly
    round about,
In silence sending forth their first petition to the
    Lord,
Then rose and formed their ranks for war, and
    marched in silence out.

What need is there to tell at length the story of the
      fight—
  How the Welshmen broke and scattered as the leaves
     before the wind,
How Cadwallon fought with fury and then swiftly
     turned to flight,
  How the sturdy English warriors were swifter still
     behind ;
How came there full accomplishment of Oswald's
     wondrous dream,
  How many miles they followed, ere to bay they
     made him turn,
How in his last despair he stood and fought beside
     the stream,
  How they left him lying headless by the side of
     Deniseburn ?

YOUNG ROLAND.

THE Scotchmen came over the Border,
 To harry Northumberland's coast :
We fought, and fell back in disorder ;
 Can a handful contend with a host ?
And Fenham's lone tower was forsaken,
 When darkest the hour of its need ;
And it fell, and young Roland was taken,
 And carried away o'er the Tweed.

Young Roland was gentle and handsome ;
 In war he could rival the best :
Yet came there no tidings of ransom,
 For his father was poor and distressed.
So he tarried, a captive and lonely,
 Like an eagle that pines to be free ;
And he thought of Northumberland only,
 And the little grey tower by the sea.

To escape not his honour was plighted ;
   He was free from the dungeon and chain :
As a wanderer untimely benighted,
   Now despairing, now hoping again,
Even so, with a heart sorrow-laden,
   Through the castle he aimlessly moved,
Till it chanced that a fair Scottish maiden
   Beheld him, and pitied, and loved.

Now Margaret was perfect in feature,
   And as good and as noble as fair ;
As though 'twere some Heavenly creature,
   She saved him from utter despair :
Her voice and her presence entrancing
   Soothed gently the tear and the groan,
Till love's light from her eyes ever glancing
   Had kindled love's light in his own.

Said the maiden, " My father is wealthy,
   His lands, they are spacious and fair :
Our love shall no longer be stealthy ;
   He shall make thee his child and his heir.

In Scotland be ever thy dwelling ;
  From her win thou honour and praise :
And bliss that is past all excelling
  Shall be ours for the rest of our days."

"Though I love thee," he answered, "with passion,
  Though fondly I yearn for thy hand,
Yet may I not win in this fashion,
  Nor barter my own native land—
Though on thee, my dear love, on thee only
  My heart is eternally set,
There's a dwelling, half ruined and lonely,
  That I may not, I cannot forget.

Though bitter the pang that must sever
  My heart, O my darling, from thee,
Yet English my soul hath been ever,
  And English it ever shall be.
Alas ! my dear love, can I press thee
  To that which myself I refuse ?
I pray God to guard thee and bless thee,
  For 'tis bitter to love and to lose."

So they parted in sorrow and yearning :
 He was freed; but O ! sore was his pain—
Yet time saw the lover returning
 To the home of his darling again.
" By darkness no more we are parted :
 King James now two sceptres doth sway."
And on maiden and youth loyal hearted
 Came at last the fair dawning of day.

BELLISTER.

"Come hither, lady bright,
Come hither, squire and knight,
Come hither all, of high or low degree :
Here is feasting in the hall,
Here is wine and cheer for all,
Here is light and laughter, mirth and minstrelsy."

Shone the torches' ample glare
O'er the noble and the fair,
O'er the warlike, o'er the winsome and the gay.
Gathered there was Tynedale's flower,
All its beauty, worth, and power,
Save one who stayed disdainfully away.

Spake the baron to the throng,
"Spare ye not the wine and song;
Let peace and laughter only reign to-night.

What though Thirlwall's sullen lord
Trusteth not my plighted word,
To-morrow shall he answer for the slight."

And he broke off with a jest;
Yet his heart was not at rest:
"Is there no healing in the hand of time?
Will he never cease to brood
On that cursed and fatal feud,
That our fathers raged and fought for in their prime?"

Rang the hall with mirth and glee,
Swelled the flood of revelry:
Yet the wine was poured, the song was sung in vain.
For the baron sat apart,
Terror gnawing at his heart,
And dark suspicion coursing through his brain.

"What meaneth he? 'Tis told
That he sitteth in his hold,
And worketh by the arts that none may tell;
That he wieldeth not the sword,
For the devil is his lord,
And his minions are the messengers of hell.

No coward I, I trow;
I can face a mortal foe;
Never fled I from the Frenchman or the Scot:
Yet the bravest cannot stand
'Gainst the fell and hidden hand
That smiteth when the victim seeth not."

And the feasters in dismay
Strove to drive his care away:
" Drink, drink, my lord, and be no more depressed !
Come, come, ye minstrels all,
Sing, as David sang to Saul:
There is gold and wine for him that singeth best."

Sang they loud of war's alarms,
Sang they softly ladies' charms,
Sang stirring ballad, merry roundelay.
But still he sat and frowned,
Nor seemed to hear a sound,
Till there came an old man clad in sober grey.

He sang, and at the strain
Rolled the long years back again;
The baron heard—his doubts and fears were gone—

Saw again that glorious fight,
When, a young and maiden knight,
He won his earliest fame at Halidon.

Up he rose and loudly cried,
" Stand thou only by my side :
Thou art the thrush ; the rest are chattering jays.
Want no more shall make thee pine,
Gold and raiment shall be thine,
And gladness cheer the evening of thy days."

Quoth the minstrel, "I am old,
Hungry, travel-worn, and cold :
I ask no meed, but only food and rest.
For thy words I thank thee well,
But to-night I cannot tell—
Till the morrow I would think on thy behest."

So they parted ; and anon
The baron's gloomy fit came on.
His name and race the harper ne'er had told.
And he asked in dire suspense
Who the singer was, and whence,
That sang so sweetly and that loved not gold.

Then a thought flashed through his mind,
"O a fool am I and blind :
This is some traitor spying for my foe :
That song, though sweet its note,
Issued from no honest throat,
Even now he worketh secretly my woe."

"Spy!"—so his brooding ran—
"If he be not worse than man,
By hellish art embodied for the task.
Some dark, foul deed I fear :
Go ye, bring the minstrel here ;
Ere he slumber, there are questions I would ask."

Forth they went the man to seek,
Back they came with pallid cheek ;
"My lord, the man is gone, and none can tell
How he vanished from the place."
Livid grew the baron's face,
For fear bites deeper than a wizard's spell.

"Seek the wretch, or all is lost !
Seek him out, nor count the cost,
And what the finder asketh, I will give.

Loose the bloodhounds on his track !
Ye must find and drag him back,
Ye must seize him, if a man of you would live ! "

Forth the cruel hounds have sprung :
Now they whimper, and give tongue,
Now, nose to earth, are tearing up the hill :
Now a shriek rings through the air,
Shriek of cursing and despair,
Rings out, and dies, and all again is still.

To their lord they bore the tale ;
But ah ! what can avail
To save the mind from horror's guilty pangs ?
Well for him if he had died
By the murdered harper's side,
Torn asunder by the bloodhounds' gory fangs.

For never from that day
Did the spectre pass away,
The awful dim grey shadow of the dead :
Did he hide or strive to fly,
Yet the ghastly thing was nigh,
Ever watching by his board and by his bed.

Stands the castle old and grey,
Slowly mouldering away,
Where Tyne turns eastward, making for the sea.
Empty is the baron's place,
Lost his name, and dead his race,
And half-forgotten e'en his memory.

Yet still there comes, 'tis said,
The grey presence of the dead
To the castle, when the storm is rising high :
Still are heard those fearful sounds,
The deep baying of the hounds,
The dying curse, the wild despairing cry.

NEVILLE'S CROSS.

[The monks of Durham are said to have watched the battle
of Neville's Cross from the Cathedral Towers.]

GREAT St. Cuthbert, wake, arise !
    For thy foes are in the land.
    Wake, and raise thy mighty hand,
And they scattered are as flies.
Unto thee lift we our eyes :
    Do thou as our champion stand.

Wasted sore with steel and fire
    Lies the land beyond the Tyne.
    Now they threaten what is thine :
Ruined lies full many a spire.
Wake, O Saint, and show thine ire !
    Will they spare thy sacred shrine ?

Help us; for, behold, the stain
  Of their rage and gluttony,
  Pillage and brutality,
Sore afflicts thy fair demesne.
Daily are thy servants slain.
  Shall they scorn a saint like thee?

See, we pray with lifted hands
  On thine Abbey's lofty heights.
  Monk must pray while warrior fights.
Guard the valour of our bands,
Guard and edge their trusty brands.
  Smite thou these Amalekites!

See thy banner waving high!
  Ah! thou takest now our part.
  May it nerve each English heart
Bravely to endure and die,
Bravely fight, and scorn to fly.
  Show thyself the saint thou art!

Come thou near, lest prayer should be
  Lost amid the battle's din.
  Lord, remember not his sin

Who shall die this day for Thee,
May he pass all blissfully
   To the crown Thy servants win.

See where Neville's charger foams !
   See where Percy's gallant band
   Battle for their wasted land,
Strike to gain their ruined homes !
Not the armies that were Rome's
   Ever made a braver stand.

See, we break, we pierce the foe !
   See, in flight they turn the steed.
   Thou art with us now indeed ;
Now we of a surety know
Thou about our path dost go,
   Thou dost help us in our need.

Holy Cuthbert ! Haste must we,
   Haste to fall before thy shrine.
   Quickly shall thine altars shine
With the gifts we owe to thee.
Soon shall all our harmony
   Tell the praises that are thine.

Though too many a widow weeps,
    Though the hills are red with gore,
    Thou hast rescued us from more,
Snatched us from more awful deeps.
Not the nobles in their keeps,
    'Tis the poor thou carest for.

Guard thou then thy people well :
    Be our refuge and our ark.
    Thou hast saved us from the dark.
Long shall high and lowly tell
How the foe before thee fell,
    That would spoil thy Haliwark.

THE MOSSTROOPERS.

To Bardon Tower eight rievers came
  From Liddesdale with lance and shield :
They set the homestead in a flame,
  When all the men were out afield ;
And ruined found we byre and bield :
  O ! but I warrant we were mad—
The thieves had fled o'er Barcom Head,
  And lifted every beast we had.

The smouldering flames were scarce put out,
  Ere neighbours' aid we sent to call ;
And soon there came an Armstrong stout,
  And soon a Ridley strong and tall.
What though our band was still too small ?
  We tracked the hoof-prints in the soil ;
" Though they be eight, we may not wait,
  If we would e'er regain the spoil."

But five were we that made the ride;
  The broad track showed the way they'd gone;
From each hill crest the moor we eyed,
  Ere to the next we galloped on.
The sun above us fiercely shone,
  Like fire it made our harness burn.
But toil and sweat must needs be met,
  And on we rode in silence stern.

And then at last we came in sight;
  They stopped as we were drawing nigh,
And six of them turned back to fight,
  And two were left to drive the kye.
So for my earliest battle I
  Couched lance, and gasped, and set my teeth;
My stout spear bent, and down I went;
  Aye, but my foe was underneath.

I drew my sword: the warm blood gushed,
  And he was lying there a corse:
And then another on me rushed,
  Ere I had time to catch my horse.

I thrust his spear aside, but force
　Of steed and rider on me bore :
I aimed a stroke, my good sword broke,
　I felt a blow, and knew no more.

I woke as though from sleep profound,
　Half dazed with lying in the sun.
Seven corpses saw I on the ground,
　Alas ! my brother's form was one.
And soon I found the fight was done ;
　I looked along the mossy track,
And joyed to see my comrades three
　Come driving all the cattle back.

To Bardon Tower came rievers eight ;
　No more for raiding they'll be fain.
Upon the moors they met their fate,
　Nor e'er saw Liddesdale again.
But woe is me for him that's slain !
　Not unavenged shall he have died.
Come sword and spear from far and near !
　We'll harry all the Scottish side.

THE PLAGUE SHIP.

THERE sailed a ship from Barbary to rob the coasts of
 Spain,
 With ninety cut-throat Moors aboard, a bloody-
  minded crew;
And through the Straits went roving forth, and o'er
 the open main
 Long time they chased, and sacked, and burnt, they
  ravished and they slew.
And oft a golden Argosy they met upon the wave,
 And every time they left behind an empty, shattered
  wreck;
Till the hold was filled with goodly bales, and many a
 Christian slave
 Lay, and cursed, and sobbed, and prayed, and died,
  and rotted 'neath the deck.

Yet they took one prize too many; for one morning it
  befell
  That they spied a noble merchantman, that neither
    fought nor fled :
And they found one man aboard her; but the Plague
  was there as well,
  And, or ever they could slaughter him, he staggered
    and was dead.
With a sound of mocking laughter on his shrivelled
  lips he died ;
  He knew that for their bloody deeds full soon would
    vengeance fall :
And each pirate muttered " Kismet," as he scrambled
  down the side,
  Too late, too late; the hand of fate had touched
    and tainted all.

Then swiftly o'er the southern sky a lurid cloud uprose,
  And swiftly rose the angry sea, and loud the tempest
    roared.
Then turned that ship of Barbary that feared no
  human foes,
  And fled away to northward from the anger of the
    Lord.

Many days to northward drave she, till her store of
  food was spent,
  With shifted cargo thumping, plunging madly by
  the head ;
Nor ever did the foaming sea and raging wind relent,
  Ere the plague brake out amongst them, and the
  half of them were dead.

But the remnant still drave onward, and at last they
  spied the land,
  The fair green shores of England : then the captain
  rose and spake,
" Come, grip once more the tiller; steer, and beach
  her on the sand :
  Inshallah, we may save our lives, although the vessel
  break."
Then steered they onward, where with lesser fury
  raged the waves,
And waited, clinging helplessly, the crisis of the
  wreck ;
And the captain bade them knock the hatches off,
  and free the slaves :
  Yet from the crowded hold but one had strength to
  reach the deck.

And he, a stout young English lad, looked up and
    saw the coast,
  And joy there fell upon him, spite of hunger, thirst,
    and pain ;
For he knew the swelling uplands of the land he
    loved the most,
  And marked the very village, where his sweetheart
    dwelt, again.
'Twas but a single glance, for swiftly came the
    moment dread,
  And rose a shriek of horror as the vessel struck the sand;
And the wild waves lashed the bodies of the dying
    and the dead,
  And all that could leapt overboard, and battled for
    the land.

Forth came the kindly village folk to them that 'scaped
    the sea,
  And came the maids and children forth, to see what
    might befall :
Then forward sprang that English lad, and shouted
    warningly,
  " Stand back ! stand back, and touch not; for the
    plague is on us all."

With thirst and hunger tortured, though he saw the
    food they brought,
  Though his father was among them, though his
    sweetheart's face he spied,
Yet stood he forth unflinchingly, nor gave his fate a
    thought,
  And spake, and fell upon the sand, and with a sob
    he died.

Back started all the villagers, and on the pirates
    frowned ;
  The maids and children shrieked and ran in terror
    at the sight :
And the Moors stood waiting idly—all but ten the
    sea had drowned—
  Stood waiting mute and weaponless, could neither
    speak nor fight.
Yet one maid there was that fled not : for awhile with
    frenzied stare
  She looked upon the lover she had loved so long
    in vain ;
Then brake from friends and kinsfolk with a cry of
    wild despair,
  And as she fell upon his corpse, Heaven joined
    their souls again.

SKOLLO THE DANE.

SKOLLO the Dane was fierce and bold,
  Fierce as a wolf, as an eagle keen ;
Skollo the Dane was grey and old,
  Seventy summers and more had seen.
" Seventy summers I've seen," quoth he ;
" Fifty have found me upon the sea,
Fighting and harrying, east and west:
Shall not this summer be like the rest ?

Am I an ox, that I thus lie still ?
  When did the wolf love the fold and stall ?
True, it is pleasant in winter's chill
  To drink and to feast in the ancient hall.
Yet when the spring hath returned again,
Loosing the sea from its icy chain,
Cometh the smell of the salt sea foam,
And base is the churl that would bide at home."

Spake the old wolf to his warriors stout,
 (Feasting they sat in the ancient hall :)
" Oft have we met at the drinking bout :
 Be this the deepest and last of all.
Drink ye, and feast ye, while lasts the night ;
Launch ye the ships with the morning's light.
Launch ye the ships, for the ocean calls
To a voyage that shall bring me to Odin's halls."

Over the sea doth the east wind moan ;
 Many a billow hath raised its head :
Over the sea have the long ships flown,
 Ringed with a bulwark of shields of red,
Sped like an arrow that flieth straight,
Arrow all heavy with death and fate,
Sped till the stout keels strike the sand,
Furrow the shores of Northumberland.

Now is there panic and flight and woe,
 Now is there pillage of church and town ;
Now through the land do the Vikings go,
 Smiting the priest by the altar down,

Slaughtering, sparing nor young nor old,
Torturing many to find their gold,
Slaying, and feasting, and slaying again :
Such were the doings of Skollo the Dane.

But, still unsated, old Skollo cried,
　" Have the fell ravens in vain been fed ?
May I not die as my sires have died ?
　Must I go home then to die in bed ?
Shall I ne'er answer to Odin's call,
Ne'er see the feast in Valhalla's hall ?
Nay, but the god craveth yet more blood,
And it shall flow in a deeper flood."

Then did his men unto Skollo speak,
　" Weary are we of thy deeds of gore :
What honour cometh of slaying the weak ?
　Wealth have we gotten in goodly store.
Surely this country is rich and thrives :
Here let us dwell, and get lands and wives.
If yet unslaked be thy thirst for gore,
Slake it thyself : we will slay no more."

Fiercely old Skollo his warriors eyed ;
   Silent he stood for awhile, amazed ;
Thrice to give vent to his wrath he tried,
   Thrice to his shoulder his axe he raised.
Then to the earth sunk the broad blade down,
Slowly relaxed the grim sea-wolf's frown,
And he heaved a sigh with a heart full sore,
He that had never heaved sigh before.

" Alas ! " quoth he, " ye are right, I trow ;
   The many must win, though it grieve the one ;
The new must come, and the old must go ;
   And the days and deeds that I loved are done.
Other are ye than the men I knew,
My warriors staunch, my comrades true.
I have lived too long ; I must voyage afar
To the place where the gods and the heroes are.

" Launch ye the *Wolf :* 'tis my last command.
   Launch ye the *Wolf*, O ye hearts of stone !
The night wind bloweth from off the land,
   And I must follow its course alone.

Tarry ye here in sloth and ease ;
Mine be the voyage and the unknown seas.
Tarry ye here on a foreign shore,
For Skollo the Dane shall ye see no more."

The night wind bloweth from off the land ;
   The ship is lost in the murky night :
The warriors linger upon the sand,
   And strain their eyes for a parting sight :
And far on the sea, like a star that blinks
O'er the ocean's edge, ere to rest it sinks,
One fiery speck upon night's dark wing
Was the last they saw of the old sea king.

www.ingramcontent.com/pod-product-compliance
Lightning Source LLC
Chambersburg PA
CBHW022204020726
47496CB00008B/2870